FiTTiNG OUT

The Cool Kid Paradox

HOW CODING HELPED ME BECOME A LUNCH BUDDY PRO

By Sarah Giles

Birch Books

For Dad

First Edition 2019

ISBN 978-1-948889-01-8

Birch Books Publishing — Washington, USA

COMPOSITION TITLE:

FITTING OUT

The Cool Kid Paradox

THIS NOTEBOOK BELONGS TO:

Max McConk

Contents

Introduction

Well, hello again! Or maybe this is hello for the first time … If that is the case and you are new here, hiya! I'm Max.

I make official reports of my adventures in being a lonely + different + shy kid in this great big world. The way things are *supposed to work* doesn't always work for me, so I am finding my own ways to do things. I call it FITTING OUT!

Instead of trying to fit *in*, I find a Max-y way to fit. If you haven't read my Friendship Experiment yet, don't worry. I'll catch you up here!

So, here's a picture of me and my best bro, Miguel.

Last summer, Miguel moved away, and I was left with a HUGE problem: no friends, and school was about to start!

I had  what to do at first. My mind went back to an old book of science experiments that I got from the library, and I thought I would give science a try. That's when I created

I went from having no ideas about how to make friends to having some not-so-great ideas.

Eventually, I figured out a trick for meeting new friends, even when I'm feeling lonely + different + shy. It's simple, really.

The secret is to just get out there and try. (And try again.) (And

try not to cry if it doesn't work at first.) (And then have a cookie.)

I found out that there are actually friend-worthy kids all over the place! If I don't see them at first, I just need to keep looking. I call it "finding my bees." Bzzzzzz!

In the end, I realized that for me, FiTTiNG OUT worked MUCH better than trying to fit in. Plus I get to be my same old, comfy self when I am with my new bros, and that is a good feeling!

After my Friendship
Experiment, it seemed like all
of my problems were over, but
whoooooaaaa, Nelly!
That was just the beginning.

So, hey, **psst!** Fitting Out
Newbies: I use a LOT of weird and
tricky words sometimes. It's one
of my quirks. See what I mean?
Quirks is a super-weird word! It
means things about my personality
that make me unique.

If I use other words that you
don't know, there are two things
you can do: First, there is a glossary
in the back of this book. Dude,
you could even check it out *now* if

you don't want to wait. Second, as you are reading, you will see this foot picture:🦶. That's a signal to head to the bottom of the page for more information. This is called a "footnote." Get it? Foot-note!

Now on to my official report on the Cool Kid Paradox! »—

Don't know this word? Check the glossary!

Footnote – Information that is placed at the bottom of the page to give additional explanation without interrupting the flow or rhythm of the text above.

CHAPTER 1:
Crushing It!

OK, here goes, I thought as I walked up to school, past the bus loop, around the flagpole, and through the double doors.

Normally, Miguel would run up, and we would hook our backpack clips together and march into school at the same time.

This year, everything was going to be different. No one to

hook into, just me. Then ... oh, thank goodness! Up ran my new friend Carlos.

"Hey, bro!" I shouted with a smile so big that I couldn't hide my excitement (and relief).

"Hey, bro! I just love that we call each other that!" said Carlos with a look of almost equal excitement.

This is AWESOME! I thought. School hadn't even started yet, and I already had someone to hang with. All my hard work last summer really paid off!

We dropped off our backpacks and met up with Cami for a couple

of rounds of two square before the morning bell. Then Woodrow was waiting for me outside Mrs. Hammersmith's classroom.

I'm *crushing it* friend-wise! Was I worried for nothing?

1st Day of School Fears:

1. Hair won't look right. IT LOOKS LIKE A BLACK MOTORCYCLE HELMET, JUST LIKE I LIKE IT!

2. I'll have to walk in front door alone. NOPE!

3. I'll have to sit alone at recess. NOT ME!

4. I won't know anyone in class. OH, BUT I DO!

5. It will be a disaster, and I'll have to run all the way home.

OH, MAN ... I REALLY HOPE THIS ONE DOESN'T HAPPEN!

As soon as I walked into the classroom, Woodrow shouted, "Hey, man!"

"Hi, Woodrow!"

"I go by Woody now."

"Since when?" I asked.

"Since last Wednesday."

"Oh, OK. I like it! Saves time," I said. "Speaking of saving time, we'd better find a seat before the morning bell, in case Mrs. Hammersmith is strict about that kind of thing."

But wait a minute now—where is Mrs. Hammersmith, anyway?

CHAPTER 2: Who ME??

It turns out that Mrs. Hammersmith was scuba diving off the coast of California, following a shiver of angel sharks.

CHECK THIS OUT: A GROUP OF SHARKS CAN ALSO BE CALLED A HERD, FRENZY, OR SCHOOL, BUT I THINK **SHIVER** IS A GOOD NAME FOR IT. THINKING ABOUT A GROUP OF SHARKS SWIMMING AROUND GIVES ME THE **CREEPS!**

Footnote

The angel shark (or angelshark) looks a lot like a stingray, with its flat body and broad fins. The angel shark's tail, though, is more sharklike, and it has gills on the side of its head instead of underneath.

Wow—Mrs. Hammersmith really IS a shark lover, just like my brother said! I thought teachers were only interested in math and stuff.

So, because of Mrs. Hammersmith's vacation, we had a substitute teacher on the first day of

school. A sub! On the first day! That almost never happens!

His name was Mr. Blank. He had white hair that stood straight up and was cut flat across the top, making a perfect straight line.

I have NO idea how he gets his hair to do that. My hair seems to have a mind of its own.

Mr. Blank started the day by telling us his story. He explained that before teaching, he worked at the US embassy in Belgium.

I don't know … I have a feeling that he might really have been a spy. Mr. Blank is a perfect spy name, don't you think?

Mr. Blank
Substitute Teacher

Mr. _____
Man of Mystery

"OK," he said. "Enough fun. Now we need to get down to business. We have a new student today, and not only is he new to this school, he is new to this town, so we're going to do what we can to help him get his feet wet."

"**HUH?**" I and four other kids asked at the same time. (I

really wanted to shout "JINX!",
but it would have been too many
jinxes to enforce.)

"'Help him get his feet wet'
means help him ease in and get
off to a good start," explained Mr.
Blank. "Kind of like when you dip
your toes into the pool to get used to
the water before jumping in."

At that moment, I felt kind of
jealous of the new kid, how he was
getting help to meet people. I didn't
have any help. I had to figure it out
for myself, and I still only know a
handful of people at this school!

Mr. Blank continued. "I want
to try something we used to do at

the embassy. When new Americans arrived to work in Brussels, they were always assigned an 'arrival guide,' someone to show them around and help them learn the lay of the land.

I think we should have three guides, one for each of the main parts of the day: classes, recess, and lunch. So, who wants to be an arrival guide?"

One hand shot straight up like a flagpole. I could only see the girl from the back, but I knew it was Sissy Gossett.

She likes to meet

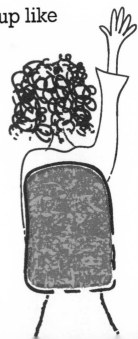

new people and LOVES to get into their business.

She is proud of the fact that she is known around school for knowing what everyone is up to. I have never talked to her before, but I'll bet she knows all about me!

"Nice! Thank you, young lady!" said Mr. Blank. "You're hired for class arrival guide duty. Now, we just need two more. Who else?"

No hands went up.

"C'mon now, don't be shy. I know for a FACT that new kids don't bite. Well, there was that one kid who ..."

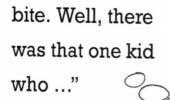

Mr. Blank's speech became quiet and turned into a low mumble that no one could hear.

He's kidding, right?

He spoke up again. "OK, well then, I guess we will leave it up to chance!"

He quickly cut some strips of paper and then walked down each aisle, dropping a cut piece of paper on each desk, skipping Sissy, of course.

"Write your name on these paper slips, bring them up to my desk, and drop them in my hat."

It took me a little longer to fill out my slip than everyone else,

since I was focused on crossing my fingers and toes for extra good luck.

Please don't pick me. Please don't pick me. It is REALLY hard to write with crossed fingers!

Mr. Blank reached into his hat and pulled out a slip. "Brayden. You've got recess duty."

Whew! Not me.

"And now, on deck for lunch duty is …" Mr. Blank reached into his hat again, pulled out a slip, and then scrunched up his face to push his eyeballs down so he could look through the bottom portion of his glasses.

The kids, who were crowded around the teacher's desk, bunched up a little closer to see if they could get a peek at what the slip said.

"It says …" Mr. Blank paused, squinting. "Matt."

Oh, SWEET mercy! Thank goodness it's not me!

Then, after a few seconds, Mr. Blank spoke up again. "Oh, ha!

Sorry, I read that wrong. I mean, Max. Max McConk."

"Ohhh, shhhaaarrrkkks!"

It was the first thing that popped into my head to say. And I found out that "sharks" is a really satisfying word to say when you're upset. *Mrs. Hammersmith would*

have been proud.

Speaking of Mrs. Hammersmith, she would NEVER have let this happen!

I realize that not very many people know me, but everyone who does know me knows that I am a keep-to-myself kind of guy. Isn't that the LAST type of person you would want to be in charge of showing a new kid around?

When I didn't know anyone, no one helped ME!

But now, somehow, it looks like MY new job will be

to help him get HIS feet wet,
   'cause HE'S new to school.

Sure, he gets wet feet, while I
   get thrown in the pool!

Mrs. Hammersmith? Rotten luck?
Who should I thank

for this first day surprise
   that we get Mr. Blank?

=18=

I'm MAD, but he's actually
  not a bad guy.

He seems kinda nice
  but, yeah, most def a SPY ...

All of the different feelings that
I was, well ... *feeling* rushed into
my brain at the same time. *Maybe
I should panic. YES, I SHOULD
DEFINITELY PANIC!*

Footnote "Def" is an abbreviation of "definitely."

CHAPTER 3:
The NEW Kid

Three sharp, loud knocks on
the metal frame of the door
to our classroom pulled me
out of my panic trance.

    The vice principal
was standing at the door
with what must have been
the new student standing in front
of her. "Come and meet your new
classmates," she said.

Whoa! I was so fascinated by what the new kid looked like that I couldn't even focus on panicking.

Wait a minute, why was the rest of the class silent? No giggling, no chatter, no jokes, no one falling out of their chair. Everyone just stood there, smiling at him like they … *knew him.*

Apparently, the new kid was a famous online video gamer named "Xan the Man." I don't know much about online video games, because I almost always use my screen time to work on my blog.

Footnote

In case you are not used to pronouncing words that start with "x," it often sounds more like a "z." So you pronounce the name Xan like you would say "Zan."

Little did I know that before Friday, I would learn what the life of this gamer was *really* like.

CHAPTER 4: The EYE of the Storm

The bell rang, and the crowd of whispering kids scattered to gather their things and head to the next class.

I took a deep breath and went over to Xan. He lowered his dark glasses just enough to look at me and then raised them back up so

that I couldn't see where he was
looking.

"All righty then. See you at
lunch," I muttered, and slunk toward
the door.

The rest of the morning went
by pretty quickly. I was so distracted
thinking about lunchtime that I
forgot to be nervous about walking
into each new class. I guess that this
was sort of a good thing.

I gazed up
   at the clock,
     missing most of gym class,

feeling closer to DOOM
   as each minute would pass.

In tech lab, we started
   on "Intro to coding."

I zoned out till
lunch just to keep
from EXPLODING.

CHAPTER 5: SHOWTIME!

Prrrrring!

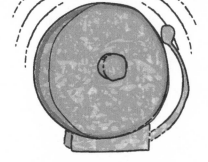

GULP! The lunch bell. It was time. I grabbed my lunchbox and shuffled to the cafeteria to meet my fate. *I hope this doesn't end with me having to run all the way home. Again.*

Xan was standing by the door and was surrounded by kids, but it was weird: no one was talking to him. It looked like there was an

invisible bubble around him and no one could get close.

Kids were talking about him, in front of him, almost as if they were visiting a statue, but no one was talking *to* him. *I wonder what Xan thinks about that.*

I stumbled up to Xan. "Sorry I'm a little late."

Xan replied, "No big."

No big what? No big deal? Yeah, that must be what he meant. No big deal. Oh, wow, and I thought abbrevs 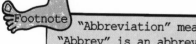 *were cool. Xan is so cool he leaves out entire words!*

"K," I said, trying to answer him back in his own language. Surely he would know that this was short for "OK," and he would recognize that I could also be very cool.

I showed Xan where to get a lunch tray and then led him through the cafeteria line.

Footnote "Abbreviation" means a shortened form of a word. "Abbrev" is an abbreviation of "abbreviation." Ha!

When it was time to get drinks,
Xan got iced green tea instead of
milk. I had never seen anyone but
the teachers get iced tea with lunch.
I know I have said this a few times
already, but, wow—this guy is so
INTERESTING!

CHAPTER 6: Trial Run

We sat down to eat, and thankfully, Woodrow—I mean *Woody*—and Carlos came over to sit with us. I was relieved, because I would be able to do my job of introducing Xan to some other kids, but I could do it with my bros, who I was already comfortable talking to.

"Carlos, Woody, this is—"

"We know, bud," interrupted

Woody. "We met him earlier in PE."

"Oh, OK," I said with a sense of defeat.

Just then, Cami rushed over, pushed Woody's lunchbox to the side, and squeezed in. She looked like she was exhausted, like she had been running an obstacle course all morning.

"Am I glad to see you guys!" she said.

"What's going on, Cami?" I asked.

"Ugh. I am having a very weird day. But I don't want to talk about it. In fact, can I just not talk at all? You guys talk. I'll listen."

"OK, but before you stop talking altogether, I have to introduce you to Xan. I am supposed to help him meet other kids, but you know … not my greatest skill!"

"Oh, um, hi. I'm Cami. My brother is a big fan of you. OK now, Cami signing off." And after that,

she said nothing else for the rest of lunch period.

I was so curious about Xan that I couldn't wait any longer. I had to ask, "So, I am not a big gamer-person. Can you tell me how everyone in the lunchroom seems to know who you are?"

"Well, I'm not a 'gamer-person,'" Xan replied. "I'm a gamer. A really good one. Every week, I play this game called TreeFort on

a live broadcast that is watched by over 100K kids."

"What are K kids?" I asked.

"No, I mean, 100K, like one hundred thousand kids. They like to repeat a couple of the things I always say when I am playing."

"Like what?" I asked.

"Like, when an enemy tries to battle me, I shout, 'NERP! Not today!' Kids love that one. Oh, and when I am about to do a really cool attack combination, I say, 'It's about to get xepic!'"

"What's xepic?" I asked.

"It's a word I made up. It's

like 'epic,'" he said in a movie announcer voice, "but MORE."

I could tell that Xan was getting annoyed that I had no idea what he was talking about.

After a few LONG minutes of silent eating, Xan said, "Well, thanks for being my lunch buddy, anyway."

"Lunch buddy?" I asked.

"That's what we used to call it at my old school. I never had to do it though. Seems awful."

"Oh, that's OK. No big," I said. This, of course, was a total lie. This was a great BIG big, especially for me!

"OK, well, if you are done eating, I guess, let's go meet some more kids," I said, trying very hard to hide the fact that I was actually pretty nervous about this. I walked in front of Xan so that he couldn't see the look of panic on my face.

OK, Max, you know how to do this. Don't overthink it. This isn't about you this time, this is just a job.

CHAPTER 7:
Buddy Duty

I walked us over to a cluster of fifth graders who I recognized from the school newspaper team.

"Um, hi," I said quietly. They kept talking. I said,

UM, EXCUSE ME, BOYS AND GIRLS.

Blech!

That made me sound like I am eighty years old.

"**Hey, guys!**" I shouted. *Much better.* "I want to introduce you to the new guy."

They finally stopped their conversation and turned around to look at us.

Xan answered exactly two questions for the school newspaper and then turned to me and said, "Can we go now?"

"Um, K." *Hmm ... that was kind of rude.*

The last few minutes of lunch went pretty much the same way. I introduced; Xan didn't say much and then wanted to get outta there.

All in all, I introduced Xan to fourteen kids. *Not too bad*, I thought.

Xan seemed bored though, like he would rather have been anywhere else than meeting these kids. He barely said anything unless

someone wanted to talk about TreeFort.

I wondered if it had gone like this with the other arrival guides or only when he was with me. *Am I doing it wrong?*

CHAPTER 8: Smooth(ish) Sailing

I did it! It's over! My gig as a lunch buddy was complete and I could go back to worrying about how I WAS going to get to know more kids at this school!

"Nice job, arrival guides!" announced Mr. Blank. "It looks like our new buddy Xan is getting the

hang of things around here. But just to be safe, why don't you guys give him a little support tomorrow too?"

BLURGH!

And just like that, I was sucked back into lunch buddy duty for another day.

The long walk home gave me plenty of time to convince myself that I could do this again. I was NOT looking forward to another lunch period of watching "Xan the Man" roll his eyes and look for the nearest exit while other kids were waiting for him to say something.

On my way home, I saw Sissy Gossett on the swings at the

playground. I desperately wanted to ask her if Xan had done the same thing when she was showing him around, or if it was just when he was with me.

Then I remembered what Pop-Pop always says: "You shouldn't be talking about anybody else's business unless you are a reporter for the nightly news." This was his way of saying, "Don't gossip."

Luckily for me, either Sissy doesn't have a pop-pop, or if she does, he doesn't say anything like that. She ran over and couldn't wait to tell me all about it.

"Oh ... my ... gosh, Max!

Can you BELIEVE Xan? WHAT is his deal? I spent all day trying to introduce him to everyone, and I mean *everyone*, and he just stood there like a mannequin!"

"Oh, really? Ha ha. Hmm … that's interesting," I said out loud, but on the inside, I had lots of things that I wanted to say.

But I didn't, because I was really trying not to

gossip. *You'd better appreciate this, Pop-Pop!*

"Well, see ya," I said as I made my escape before all of my feelings poured out. But oh my gosh! Did you hear that? It's not just me!

Something is going on with Xan. I wonder why he doesn't want to make new friends. Are we not cool enough? Maybe he has so many friends online that he doesn't need any more?

Hmph, I guess tomorrow will be very much like today. At least I know what to expect! And get this—I am getting kind of used to talking to new people now! Like

Sissy Gossett, I talked to her with no problem. Man oh man, I am getting good at this!

I was almost home when I passed a green house on the corner with a moving truck in the driveway.

Uh-oh, this must be Xan's house. Yikes—I'd better run by before he sees me, or else I'll have to say hello, and I really don't know what to say after that ...

I started to sprint and had just begun to pick up some real speed when I heard a jingling chain. I looked up and saw a huge brown bear charging toward me.

Aaaaahhhh!!

K, so it turns out it wasn't
a bear but a really large brown
dog. Still, I was so startled by the
charging giant that I lost my balance
and fell onto my back in the grass.
Oofta!

Before I could get back up, the

big dog galloped over and put two
huge, soft paws right on my chest
and started licking my face with its
enormous, sticky tongue.

So much for going incognito.
A lady ran out of the green house.
"Awesome, no! Awesome, get
down!"

Xan's dog's name is AWESOME?

"Hey, bud. You OK?" she asked kindly. "Oh, your elbow is bleeding. Let me at least give you a bandage!"

My mom was on her way from work and happened to see me lying in the yard in front of the green house. She pulled her car over to the side of the street and stopped with a SCREEEECH!

She jog-walked over to me with a confused look on her face. (I am sure she wanted to run over, but it is not possible to run with fancy work shoes on.)

"Max—oh my gosh! What are

you doing, lying around in our new neighbor's yard?"

Mom turned to introduce herself to the woman, and I was formally introduced to Awesome.

As I got up to brush myself off, I noticed a shadow in the window … I recognized its signature hairstyle. I waved to Xan.

"Why don't you guys come inside, and we'll get him fixed up?" said the woman (who I now realized was probably Xan's mom), and she led us into their house.

CHAPTER 9: Behind the Scenes

As soon as we walked through the front door of Xan's house, I saw the most AMAZING room I have ever seen in someone's house before.

There was a desk with three huge video screens, a spotlight, and a camera. Tucked in front of it was

a tall, skinny chair with a very high back that looked like it belonged in the cockpit of a spaceship. Draped over the back of the chair was a set of headphones that had a little round microphone piece attached to it.

Xan's mom told us to wait in the hall while she got her first aid kit. She pushed Xan toward me by his shoulders and gave him a look, urging him to say hi to me ... *or else!*

"Whoa! Is this your mom's office?" I asked.

Xan answered, "No. This is *my* office. This is where I broadcast from. I sit here and play TreeFort, and the camera sends the video out over the internet. Do you wanna try it?"

"No, thanks. I'm not really into video games. Very cool though!"

"Wow, I don't know any kids who aren't into video games! You are

one weird dude, Max McConk."

"Thanks!" I said with a smile. I have decided that *weird = interesting*, so I always take it as a compliment.

Xan snapped back with "Well, if you don't want to play, I guess you can leave now."

Whoa! What just happened?

"Sorry," Xan continued. "It's just that it's my birthday on Friday, and even though you and Sissy and Brayden introduced me to all of those kids, I don't have anyone to invite to my party except the three of you.

"So there. You're invited." Xan rolled his eyes so far up that I saw his eyeballs pop up above his dark glasses for just a second.

"Wait a minute! This is great!" I almost shouted.

Xan's eyebrows dropped below his glasses. "I tell you that I don't have anyone to invite to my party, and you think this is great?

You really ARE weird."

"Thanks! What I mean is that the party gives you something to help 'break the ice' with the kids at school. And I am no expert on people, but from what I saw today … there's major ice."

"What are you talking about?"

"Don't take this the wrong way, Xan," I answered, "but when I introduced you to the other kids, you seemed kind of … mean."

"But I wasn't being mean, Max. I just didn't know what to say, so I didn't say anything. I just don't get it. I should have a ton of friends! At least enough for a party.

Thousands of kids watch me play TreeFort. Look how many hearts I have collected on my GamePage profile!"

GamePage

Xan the Man
TreeFort Master Champion.
LIVE broadcast every Wednesday
💜 **133,121**

Tune in to watch the legendary TreeFort master build, climb, and shred his way to the top of the trees, unlocking challenge levels.

"But, Xan, think about it," I said. "Do you want kids to 'heart' you, or do you want kids to *get*

to know you? Besides, you don't collect friends, you make them," I said. "And my opinion is, you don't even need that many. For some people, a couple of good ones is all they really need.

"Maybe you just need to try it and see. And maybe lose the dark glasses," I suggested.

"You don't get it, Max. Kids think they know me because they have seen my videos, but if they got to know the *real kid* behind 'Xan the Man,' they would be disappointed with how ordinary I am."

"But you're a cool kid," I told him. "I thought cool kids didn't have trouble with this kind of stuff."

"I'm not a cool kid," Xan answered. "I'm just a kid who's good at something. I think that's the problem. People expect me to be cool, but I'm just me. I don't know what I'm *supposed* to be like."

This really got my mind going. Now I was rethinking

everything. *What makes a cool kid, anyway ... and who decides?* I was starting to realize there was probably more than one kind of cool ...

"What did you talk about with your friends back home?" I asked.

"Well, I didn't talk to that many people, but I chatted with viewers every night."

"What do you mean, like chat on the phone?" I asked.

"No, *Grandpa*, like text through the GamePage app," Xan replied.

"Oh, I get it," I said. *Did he just call me Grandpa?* "I mean, did you

talk with anyone, like chat ... with your mouth?" I realize that this was probably a totally "Grandpa" way to say this too, but I really couldn't figure out a different way to ask it.

Xan started up again. "Unless we are talking about TreeFort, I don't know what to talk about. So, no, I didn't *really* talk to that many people ... with my mouth. What am I supposed to talk about, anyway?"

"I don't know," I answered.

"That's a big help. Thanks a lot," Xan said sarcastically.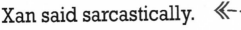

Ooh! Super–big, super–weird word here! Check the glossary to find out the meaning!

"No, I mean I really don't know," I explained. "I am the expert on me, but YOU are the expert on you. Just be yourself. It's the easiest thing to be!"

"This is different. I'm different. No one has the same problem as me."

"I hear ya, Xan. You may not realize this, but I, too, am quite different."

"Oh, really?" Xan said, sarcastically again.

"Yes, really! And I DON'T have an easy time making friends with people. I just figured out the ME way to do it."

"What do you mean?" Xan asked.

"The regular old way of doing stuff may work if you are a regular old kid, but if you aren't a regular kid, you have to find what works for you. Trust me, I know what I'm talking about here. I had to use science to help me, for gosh sakes!"

"But I'm not good at science. It's my worst subject."

"Well, what's your best subject, then?" I asked.

"Hmm ... I guess it would be coding," Xan answered. "It just

makes sense to me, like a video game. All you have to do is tell the computer to do what you want it to do."

"OK then, let's solve this problem with coding."

"What do you mean?" Xan asked. "I've used coding to make my own video game before, but how do I use it to save my birthday party?"

"Let me work on it tonight, and I'll explain the rest at lunch tomorrow," I said, trying to hide my excitement about starting a new project.

CHAPTER 10:
The Paradox

Talking to Xan really got my mind
going. A famous kid with thousands
of fans can't scrape together
enough kids for a birthday party?
What a paradox!

PARADOX:

A situation, thing, or person
that happens to be completely
different from what you might
expect or think would be true.

That sounds like
Xan for sure!

Xan the Man has Ks
 of fans under his spell.

Xan the kid needs help
 making friends IRL.

I'm doing my best
 to help him, but, DUDE!

How to get past his
 TOO-COOL attitude?

I tried to remember what
the teacher said about coding in
technology lab today, but I was so
nervous about being an arrival guide
that I totally spaced out.

Mom's a developer. I should
ask her. I am not sure exactly what a

developer does, but I know it has something to do with computers.

Mom explained to me that coding = computer programming.

She said, "Everyone thinks it's complicated, but it really just means learning the language and giving the computer instructions to get it to do what you want it to do. You've already done it before, Max."

"I have?"

"Yes, every time you and Dad program your robot, Switches, to do something—that's coding!"

Footnote
It turns out that a developer is someone who writes computer programs (code) as their main job. SCORE!

```
SWiTCHES DANCE iNSTRUCtiONS
>BEGIN 'Pattern'
        >"hands"; move=left AND
                >"hips"; tilt=right
                :behind hands
        >"hands"; move=right AND
                >"hips"; tilt=left
                :through hands
        >REVERSE
        >"hands"; move=right AND
                >"hips"; tilt=left
                :behind hands
        >"hands"; move=left AND
                >"hips"; move=right
                :through hands
        >REVERSE
>REPEAT 'Pattern' until music ends
```

Mom went into the kitchen,
scribbled a note, and handed it to
me with a chocolate zucchini
muffin.

MOM'S SECRET MUFFIN
RECIPE IS HIDDEN BEHIND
THE GLOSSARY. SHHHH!

From the desk of MELINDA M^cCONK

BASIC CODING:

1. Learn the language of the device that you want to talk to.

2. Next, write instructions in that language for what it should do.

3. Try out your instructions in a safe testing mode.

4. Now it's time to "go live" and release your new code.

Oh, and remember to be efficient! Don't try to put anything extra in the code. It just wastes energy and can cause unpredictable results. Just keep it simple, and focus on steps that will lead to the result you are looking for.

GOOD LUCK, SWEET BOY!!

CHAPTER 11: The "Real Kid" Code

"I don't know about this," Xan said when we met up the next day for lunch. "This is weird, using coding to make friends. It's just weird."

"Thanks!" I said back. "Now, here's my plan. To teach my robot, Switches, how to dance, my dad and I had to enter the right code into his brain module.

"First, we had to learn the language. Then we had to give clear instructions for what we wanted Switches to do. The only way we knew if we got the command right was to try it out.

"By following the same steps, we could *code* the kids at school to get to know the real you. When you only show them 'Xan the famous gamer,' who doesn't say much and is too cool to hang out and talk, you are programming them to think of you that way.

"Maybe you just need to give other kids the information they

need to dance, er … I mean, to see you the way you *really* are. Once you see that they want to hang out with the REAL you, you can invite them to your party.

"One warning: when you first meet someone, they won't have time to listen to your whole life story. You have to be efficient."

"OK. I've got no idea what 'efficient' means," Xan admitted.

"Basically, stick to a few important highlights that you think really show who you are," I explained.

How to code 5th grade kids

1. Learn the language.

Today, when Brayden and Sissy are showing you around, pay attention to what they tell you about the other kids. Listen to what other kids say about themselves too.

2. Write instructions.

Write down 1-2 questions you could ask a kid about themselves. My friend Miguel did this to get me to start talking, and now we are best bros! Next, write down a few things that you want people to know about you, and memorize them. Then, all you need to do is decide which thing to say at what time.

3. Test the code.

You can practice on me! I'll be riding my uni 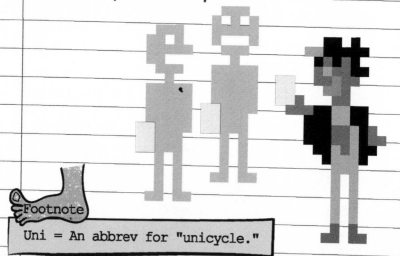 at the park after school. You can come by there and try out some of the things you want to say.

4. Go live!

Tomorrow, at morning recess, see if you can talk with someone for a bit. If it is going well, invite them to your party.

Xan and I spent the whole lunch break planning out how he would use his "code" to help him make *real* friends. As we were finishing up, I felt like it was a good time to try out a new, custom-made rhyme on Xan.

To make real friends OFFline,
    you will have to unplug.
Write your code in REAL mode,
    and then test and debug.
Listen and THEN talk—
    that's the way to connect.
I'll bet friends are more fun
        to HAVE than collect.

CHAPTER 12: Xan with a Plan

That afternoon, Xan met me in the park, and I helped him write down some things he could say. I organized his questions and details into an official bio.

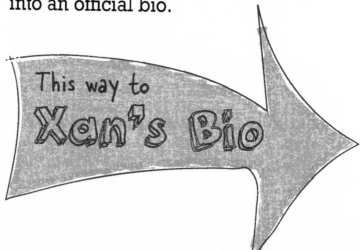

This way to Xan's Bio

Official Bio & MASTER PLAN!
"Xan the Man" (aka Alexander Harris)

His name's Alexander,
       but he goes by Xan.
To solve his BiG problem,
       he needs a BiG plan.

Ask questions, get them talking—
       that's how to begin.
(And BONUS: this takes some of
       the pressure off him!)

Listen, pay attention to what
       they say, and then
throw in some REAL Xan facts, and
       BOOM! New friend. The end.

 # XAN FACTS

Yes, he's good at TreeFort, but he wants to confess:

1. He wishes he knew magic and how to play chess.

2. He likes to read. A LOT. (Oh my gosh, just like me!)

3. He started drinking green tea the year he turned three. (Decaf, of course.)

= 80 =

4. His favorite lunch is his mom's vegan chili.
(I've always been more of a phở person really.)

Yum!

5. He thinks old 80s movies are an absolute blast.

6. It's not the first time he's moved, and it won't be the last.

7. He likes ALL KINDS of games, not video only.

8. His mom works a lot, and he gets kinda lonely.

Footnote: Phở is a Vietnamese soup, often consisting of stock, noodles, and meat. Many people say "phở" wrong. It is pronounced like "fuh," the same "u" sound as in "yum!"

I walked home from the park, feeling like I should pat myself on the back for a job well done. I had helped another kid learn the "Max Method" to making friends. I bet I could make a million bucks with this idea!

This good feeling continued all the way into the next school day ... until morning recess. I stopped in my tracks when I saw Xan looking just as "too cool" as ever.

What? What about the plan? What about the code?

He was standing at the zip line ladder, passing out invitations to everyone who walked up to him.

He didn't say anything to anyone.
He just gave out the papers. After
a while, kids
were lining up
just to see what
he was giving
out.

I have to
admit I was
peeved! I wasn't
ready to talk to Xan
about it and let him know
how I felt about the fact that he
totally bailed on the plan that we
had spent most of yesterday talking
about.

After recess, when Woody

sat down next to me in class, I noticed that he was clutching one of the papers in his hand. I read the invitation from top to bottom to see if I could get any clues as to what in the world Xan was thinking.

GAME-A-PALOOZA

It's about to get XEPiC! It's Xan's birthday, and we're celebrating with games, games, and MORE games!

WHEN: This Friday at 6 p.m.

WHERE: Xan's house

Ugh! "Xan the Man" is worse than before. He is not going to let anyone see past the fact that he is a video game champion.

What is a game-a-palooza, anyway? Do we all just sit around and watch "Xan the Man" be "Xan the Man"?

Oh, great, I thought, sarcastically.

Oh, no! Now I'm being sarcastic! "Xan the Man" is rubbing off on me! Am I gonna become more like him now? NERP! Not today!

CHAPTER 13: Game-a-palooza

I was not looking forward to seeing "Xan the Man" float any further away from the real world. I went to his party anyway, because to be honest, he is the first person besides Miguel that ever invited me to a party. Please don't tell anyone that. It's embarrassing.

When Mom pulled up to Xan's house, we saw a huge banner

outside that said "Game-a-palooza."

"Wow!" said Mom. "This looks like it is going to be mega-fun!"

"Yeah, yeah, I'm sure it'll be xepic," I said, sarcastically again! Blech! This is not very Max-y. I gotta break this habit!

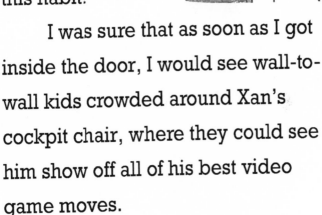

I was sure that as soon as I got inside the door, I would see wall-to-wall kids crowded around Xan's cockpit chair, where they could see him show off all of his best video game moves.

I took in a slow breath and

walked up to the green house. I was feeling as excited about this party as I would be about a big pile of homework.

When Xan's mom opened the door, I didn't see anyone inside. And Xan's office was dark. The screens were off, and no one was in there. *Aah! Oh no! Nobody came to the party?* I started to feel sad for Xan.

"Hi, Mrs. Harris. Where is everyone?" I asked.

"Oh, they're out back. I'll show you, hon." Xan's mom replied.

She led me through the kitchen to the backyard. I started to hear

people-ish noises and was relieved to see that maybe it wasn't as sad as I had thought.

No, it was actually pretty great! I saw at least thirty kids from school, running around the yard with colored jerseys with numbers on them.

Xan's Game-a-palooza was not a video game watch-a-thon after all. "Game" meant yard games. There was an obstacle course, dodgeball, even tug-of-war! The kids from school were having a regular old good time at the party, and Xan now seemed just like a regular old kid.

And the kids from school had no trouble at all hanging out with a regular old kid. Our real-kid code was live ... and it was working!

Xan sat next to me while we were having cake. (I guess he had gotten used to sitting next to me when it was time to eat.)

"How did you come up with this party plan so fast, Xan?" I asked.

"Well, after you left yesterday, I thought more about the coding idea and decided that it might be easier to program lots of kids all at once. You know, more efficient.

"You know, Max, the fact that you figured out your own way to get

stuff done and showed me how to find mine is actually very ... cool."

And then it happened: he smiled. Xan smiled! I realized that I had never seen him smile before. I took this to mean that our coding project was a success.

CHAPTER 14: Conclusion

YES! Another project complete! Xan and I figured out that coding is great for more than just computer games and programs. Basically, we discovered that you can code how people see you by what you decide to show.

Xan was able to get kids to see him as a real kid, by showing them that he is, well … a real kid!

Here's another BIG thing I learned from my time as an arrival guide: It turns out that you don't have to be the strongest, friendliest, or coolest kid to make a difference in someone else's life. Anyone can help someone!

And **BONUS:** helping Xan made me totally forget to be nervous during the first week of

school!

Then there is the other side of the story to think about: last summer, I thought I was, like, the only almost-ten-year-old who didn't know how to make friends, but maybe it's a more common problem than I thought.

I guess maybe everyone needs help sometimes ... even the cool ones, like *us.*

Making REAL friends takes work,
whether on– or offline.

I think true friends are made
one REAL chat at a time.

YOU KNOW. LIKE,
WITH YOUR MOUTH.

GLOSSARY

(The words are in the same order that you see them in the book.)

Paradox – A situation, thing, or person that happens to be completely different from what you might expect or think would be true.

US embassy in Belgium:

US embassy – The headquarters for representatives of the United States government serving in another country.

Belgium – A small country in Western Europe, with a border on the North Sea.

Trance – Being in a daze or stupor, like someone who is sleepwalking or has been hypnotized.

Blog – A website containing entries of the writer's own thoughts, opinions, and experiences.

Mannequin – A large doll or human statue with poseable arms, legs, and head (if it has one—some mannequins are headless!) that is often used to display clothing.

Gossip – If you don't know this one, hopefully, it is because you don't do it! Talking about rumors or someone's private matters to others.

Sprint – When you run as fast as you can but for a short distance.

Incognito – Going unrecognized; no one can tell that it's you.

Sarcastic – A type of harsh humor where someone says the opposite of what's true in an exaggerated way to make fun of the idea.

Chocolate Zucchini Mini-Muffins

- 1/2 cup white sugar
- 1/4 cup light brown sugar
- 1/2 cup unsweetened applesauce
- 2 egg whites
- 1 teaspoon vanilla extract
- 1 1/4 cup flour
- 1/4 cup unsweetened cocoa powder
- 1 teaspoon baking soda
- 1 cup grated zucchini
- 1 cup semi-sweet chocolate chunks

Preheat oven to 350°F.

In large bowl, mix sugar, applesauce, egg whites, and vanilla with an electric mixer until combined.

In separate bowl, mix flour, cocoa, and baking soda. Gradually add dry ingredients to sugar mixture and mix just until combined. *Do not over mix*

Stir in zucchini and chocolate chunks.

Scoop batter into greased mini-muffin tin. Bake 13 minutes. Makes 24 mini-muffins.

BONUS: Cami's first day of school.

LAST YEAR—WHEN WE HAD A NEW SUBSTITUTE TEACHER

This is how it used to be for me. I was an ordinary, unremarkable, and totally forgettable what's-her-name. No one looked for me; no one asked what I thought. When kids told stories, I was never a character in them.

I wasn't lonely though. I had my brother and a couple of friends from the neighborhood.

I spend a lot of time in my own head, sort of narrating what I am doing, so that at least someone recognizes that I am on this planet, even if it's just me. *Writing in this journal now. Chewing watermelon gum.*

I used to daydream that I was a ghost of a girl who didn't know she was a ghost, so she was going through her regular routine, not realizing that she was invisible to  the people around her.

Having a quiet breakfast in the kitchen. Riding my skateboard to school. Zombie-walking from one class to the next. Riding home. But no one in the real world even knew I was there.

Once, my sneaker slipped on the cafeteria floor, and I fell backward, right onto my bum. I was holding on tight to my lunch tray, so when I hit the ground, the impact sent my silverware flying into the air, only to land on a nearby table, rattling like a tambourine until it finally settled.

Everyone, and I mean EVERYONE, stopped to laugh or clap. Why do they always clap?

After that, my daydream vanished, and I remembered that I was indeed NOT a ghost, I was only *nearly* invisible. Sadly, not invisible enough

to escape this dreadful lunchroom
fiasco.

Eventually, I stopped caring
that people only barely noticed me. I
just went through the motions of my
regular routine.

Breakfast, skateboard, school,
skateboard, dinner, sleep. Kids didn't
pick me for their teams. *Breakfast,*
skateboard, school, skateboard, dinner,
sleep. Kids didn't care what my
favorite graphic novel was. *Breakfast,*
skateboard, school, skateboard, dinner,
sleep. Teachers didn't pick my raised
hand out of the sea of other raised
hands. *Breakfast, skateboard, school,*

skateboard, dinner, sleep.

Things had been this way as long as I could remember.

Today was the first day of school, and I didn't expect it to be any different. Breakfast, skateboard, school. The first half of my ordinary school day was off to its ordinary start (except that my first-day-of-school jeans had shrunk in the wash, so that I could feel a cool breeze on my ankles).

Blurgh! The

outfit that I had carefully picked out this summer was already messed up! Then, *sigh,* I didn't really care anymore. No one would be looking at me, anyway.

Opening double doors. Kids everywhere. Wait, something was different ... Oh no, this is it—the ghost thing is really happening!

Had I been bitten by an exotic mosquito and caught malaria? Did I run into a garbage truck on my way to school?

Tripped over some kid's green cowboy boots and fell onto hands and knees.

Nope, I'm real. I felt every embarrassing and hand-stinging moment of that fall.

What was it, then? Everything looked strange ... looked *little* somehow.

When I got to my new fifth-grade classroom, I headed for my new fifth-grade desk, ready to settle into the background for the rest of the year.

But it wasn't a *new* desk: I thought I'd gotten a weird *old* desk, because my knees were grazing the underside of the desktop. And I could see all the way to the front of the class even though I was on the back row behind three other kids.

Once the bell rang and everyone took their seats, I figured out what was going on.

I was TALLER than every single kid in the class! I knew I had grown a little taller since last year, but my brother had too. Probably everyone had. I hadn't realized that I had grown almost three inches, just in August alone!

All of a sudden, I ... stood ... out! When you looked around the room, I was the FiRST one you saw.

Everyone in the class noticed too. In clusters of two or three at

a time, they all came over to tell me
what they thought about this change.

I was stunned by the attention.
I felt like I had gotten a punch in the

nose. *Eyes stinging, watering.* I went from being invisible to having nowhere to hide!

But it was more than that. It was like there was a white-hot spotlight on me, blinding me from seeing the audience of kids watching me, waiting to hear what I would say next.

This was incredible ... and terrifying! A huge opportunity ... and responsibility. I had to make these next words count.

Not "Chameleon" anymore. Nowhere to hide. This was my chance to take up a whole new place in the world. Kids want to know what I am all about! *What do I tell them?*

Thinking about where to start. OK, I got it. *Clearing throat. Opening mouth ...*

Read more of Cami's story at the end of FITTING OUT Book #3!

Acknowledgments

For pouring their expertise, advice, and support into this work, I wish to thank:

Editorial: Leonora Bulbeck for perfectly sewing up the fine details, and Rachel Cone-Gorham for painting the big picture.

Layout and Design: Catherine Heinz and Jason Heinz for indispensable advice on what to add AND where.

Alpha-Beta Readers: Courtney Loquasto and Ashley Giles for having the guts to shoot me straight and challenge me in the very best way.

Junior-Betas (in alphabetical order): Ally, Anna, Beckett, Brayden, Cael, Emery, Finn, Michael, and Shaun for fearlessly sharing your opinions and ideas to help make sure my stories are funny and kid-worthy.

A special thank-you also to:

Dear family and friends for so much cheerleading, sail-filling, and, when needed, fire-lighting.

My moms for carrying my books around in their purses, just in case they encounter someone who hasn't read them yet.

All of the readers, parents, educators, and librarians who have invited Max's stories into their hearts, homes, classrooms, and libraries.

About the Author:

This is a photo of Sarah Giles when she was in third grade, making her favorite funny face. Why? Because it makes her laugh. Wearing a leotard instead of a shirt. Why? Because it's fun. And all the while, not caring a bit what anyone else might think about that.

She thinks of that time in her life as the golden age of joy, creativity, and fearless ME-dom.

Books in the FiTTiNG OUT series

1. The Friendship Experiment

2. The Cool Kid Paradox

3. The Nitpicker's Dilemma

Switches and Peeps have
their own books too!

Perfect for readers
ages 6-8.

SWiTCHeS and PEEPS
Man's Best FriendS

#1 MBF

Sarah Giles

Made in the USA
Middletown, DE
23 September 2020